Helpful Betty

solves a mystery

For Emily—MK

To Annette and Sally,

both helpful—MM

Helpful Betty

solves a mystery

Story by Michaela Morgan
Illustrated by Moira Kemp

Betty likes to be helpful.

One day, while she is tidying

the jungle,

she finds a magnifying glass.

"Aha!" says Betty.

"Now I can be an ace detective.

All I need is a mystery."

So off she goes,

looking high and low,

looking for a mystery to solve,

when all of a sudden,

she finds ...

an egg.

"A poor lost motherless egg,"

says Betty.

"How did it end up here?

It's a mystery.

Aha! A mystery!

This is a case for helpful me!"

And she's off,

thundering and blundering,

tracking and trailing,

looking for a home

for the poor lost egg.

"But Betty," says the frog,

"it belongs to that . . ."

But Betty is busy.

Too busy to listen.

Busy looking here and there,

until

all of a sudden

she finds . . .

a nest.

"Aha!" says Betty.

"A nice comfy nest

for this poor lost egg.

All I need now is

a mom to take care of it."

And she's off again,

sniffing and snooping,

dashing and crashing,

looking for a mom

to take care of the egg.

"But Betty," says the frog,

"look!"

"I *am* looking!" says Betty.

"I'm looking high and low,

I'm looking here and there,

I'm looking everywhere!"

"But Betty," says the frog,

"don't you see . . ."

And then,

all of a sudden,

Betty finds . . .

the river.

She also finds a bird.

"Lose an egg?" asks Betty.

"No," says the bird.

"I laid three eggs,

I hatched three eggs,

and now I have three babies.

But one of them is . . .

a monster!

It's cranky and it's snappy.

It can't sing—it just croaks.

And fly? It won't even try.

How could an egg of mine

turn out like this?

It's a mystery!"

"I've got a mystery too,"

says the crocodile.

"I laid one egg,

and one egg hatched,

but now I have . . .

one wimp!

It's soft and it's fluffy.

It eats like a bird.

And swim? It won't even try.

How could an egg of mine

turn out like this?

That's a mystery!"

"More mysteries! Let me

help!" cries Betty.

"I'm an ace detective,

and I'm an ace swimming

teacher, too.

I'll teach your baby to swim."

And she's off,

muddling and meddling,

boasting and bragging,

swaggering and swimming,

until . . .

SNAP! go some very sharp teeth,

and YEOWCH! Betty jumps,

and "WHEE! I'm flying!"

says a little cheeping voice.

"Now, *that's* my baby!"

says the bird.

Then "WHEE! I'm swimming!"

says a little croaking voice.

"Now, that's *my* baby!" says the

crocodile. "Betty, you've done it.

But how?"

"It's a mystery to me,"

says Betty,

and she's off again,

still looking, always looking,

for someone she can help.

This edition first published 1994 by Carolrhoda Books, Inc.
Produced by Mathew Price Ltd, Old Rectory
House, Marston Magna, Yeovil, Somerset BA22 8DT, England

Carolrhoda Books, Inc. c/o The Lerner Group
241 First Avenue North, Minneapolis, MN 55401

Library of Congress Cataloging-in-Publication Data

Morgan, Michaela.
    Helpful Betty solves a mystery / by Michaela Morgan ; illustrated by
Moira Kemp.
        p.   cm.
    Summary: Helpful Betty the hippopotamus finds a magnifying glass
while tidying up the jungle and goes looking for a mystery to solve.
    ISBN 0-87614-832-1
    [1. Hippopotamus—Fiction.   2. Helpfulness—Fiction.   3. Eggs—
Fiction.]   I. Kemp, Moira, ill.   II. Title.
PZ7.M8255Hd   1994
[E]—dc20   93-39050
                                                                                   CIP
                                                                                    AC

Printed in Hong Kong
Bound in the United States of America
1 2 3 4 5 6 – I/OS – 99 98 97 96 95 94